The Cat Who Came By Plane

Written and Illustrated by

Hannelore U. Ramanayake

ISBN: 978-1-954095-79-3

The Cat Who Came By Plane

Illustrated by Hannelore U. Ramanayake.

For permission requests, write to the publisher at the address below.

Yorkshire Publishing
1425 E 41st Pl
Tulsa, OK 74105
www.YorkshirePublishing.com
918.394.2665

Published in the USA

For my granddaughter Alysha,
because of whom I fell in love
with illustrated children's books
...and who believed that
I could do this!

Tigger, a handsome gray
and black tabby cat,
looked lazily out of the window.

His house was on a
busy street in a small
Pennsylvania town.

He had a family of owners: Grandma, Grandpa, Jacqui, and her little girl, Alysha. They loved Tigger dearly and wanted to keep him safe and beautiful. He was well cared for; pampered would be the more accurate word. Therefore, he was an "inside" cat.

Day after day, Tigger sat at the window and watched fluttering birds or drifting leaves. In winter, the snowflakes really fascinated him. He often tried to catch them, but all he could do was touch the glass that separated him from the "real" world. Once in a while a stray cat would jump on the porch to visit Tigger. They hissed and purred at each other. But always through the glass.

Surely there must be more to life than eating,
drinking, sleeping, and watching the world through a
glass? True, he was comfortable and safe. He knew
he was loved. But why couldn't he explore outside?

One summer a scary thing happened: Tigger was taken to the vet, given a shot, put into a box, and handed over to a stranger who put him into a dreadfully noisy machine.

What on earth had happened? Where were his owners? After being such a good and obedient pet, had they now abandoned him or given him away? Question upon scared question went through Tigger's mind. All these strange noises and strange people handling his cage frightened him. Though, most were really nice and treated him well. His cage boasted the letters V I P in bold print.

After endless hours of being tossed around and loaded from one noisy machine into another, Tigger was on the ground again. There were many new smells, strange noises, and long times alone in the cage. Tigger cried loudly and persistently until he heard a familiar voice.

"Hey, Tigger, welcome to Oklahoma," said a cheery voice. The cage was lifted into a car and he saw them. Grandma and Grandpa had come to take him to his new home!

live your dream

18

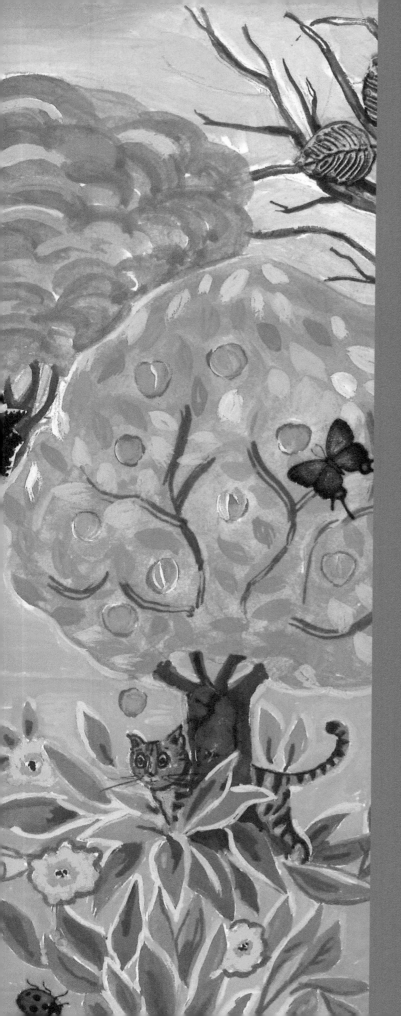

And what a home it was! Tigger had never been in a large house with a big garden. It was fantastic, full of possibilities, but also very scary.

The only way to
cope was to hide
for a couple of days
in the bedroom.

Everything was new and different. There was a large, mean looking dog in the house. This fear-inducing beast by the name of Hershey only wanted to chase Tigger.

Hershey's chance came a few days later when Tigger took his first cautious steps into the garden. Hershey went straight after him.

Petrified, Tigger raced up a tree.
Not being used to such strenuous
activity and being rather fat due to
his comfortable life in Pennsylvania.

Tigger ripped out one of his claws,
and fell out of the tree,
but he managed to escape the dog.

Hershey was not the only problem;
the birds didn't like Tigger either.
They did not want their little babies
to be eaten by a cat. Every time poor
Tigger tried to sunbathe, the mockingbirds
would dive and pick his fur.

On a dark day like this, Tigger would woefully think back to his old and comfortable life in Pennsylvania. Wouldn't it have been better to have stayed? Why did his owner have to take him away from all that was cozy and comfortable?

One day, however,
Tigger ventured out,
met a neighbor's cat,
and chased a mole
and then a mouse.
He decided life here
was not so bad after
all and soon become
the adventurous
cat he had always
dreamed of being.

To his great delight, Anni, a black lab
with a gentle nature, replaced Hershey.

Tigger was not exactly thrilled with this addition, but he established his lordship quickly, and life became manageable.

The new beginning was tough for an old cat. On his tenth birthday, the smile on his face was proof that he was one happy, fulfilled, and contented cat. He knew he was loved by his family, respected by the birds, and feared by mice and moles of the neighborhood. He enjoyed long naps during the day and protected his family from rats and creepy crawlies at night.

He was as handsome as ever but not in the soft, pampered way from days gone by. A ripped ear and some missing whiskers were proof of real-life encounters.

Gone are the days of watching life through a glass window!

Acknowledgements

Thank you to my family who lived the true tale of Tigger with me, and who have listened to every version of the story I have written! Thank you to my positive friends, who kept on pushing me forwards, and my negative friends, who were convinced that this would never work; both made me dig in my heels! Thank you to Alysha, who definitely never gave up and was a great help with editing and computer work.

I am thankful for the Scripture that underpinned this story.

Jeremiah 29:11 "For I know the plans I have for you," says the Lord, "They are plans for good and not for evil, to give you a future and a hope."

Lightning Source UK Ltd.
Milton Keynes UK
UKHW051153131121
393861UK00002B/94

9 781954 095793